GAMEMASTER

GAMEMASTER

ROBERT PETER JACOBY M.S.

INKWELL PRODUCTIONS

A SPECIAL THANKS ...
to Nick Ligidakis,
Patricia, Paul, Sophia, Inkwell Productions
and the amazing spirit of the members of the
Self-Publishers Group in Scottsdale, Arizona.
Your vision to help restore peace and harmony in our
world were the catalysts for starting this work.
Your support and wisdom gave me the courage
in bringing this dream to life.
Your unconditional love gave me the strength
to see it through.
I am forever grateful,
and eternally thankful.

Peace and love always,
Robert

ॐ

To The Eternal One, thank you for Love.

To my Mother and Father,
I love you.
I treasure all that you have taught me,
and still teach me to this day.

To all of my dear friends,
thank you for all of your Laughter,
Love, and most of all support and patience
over the years.
I treasure *every* moment together.

To Neli,
thank you for reminding me how to listen
and above all for teaching me the
instrumental art of flying.

By Robert P. Jacoby
rjacoby@gamemaster4ever.org
www.gamemaster4ever.org

First Printing March 2002

ISBN 0-9718155-2-6

Published by
INKWELL PRODUCTIONS
3370 North Hayden Rd. #123-276
Scottsdale, Arizona 85251

Tel.	480-315-9636
Fax.	480-315-9641
Toll Free	800-214-3550
E-mail	INFO@INKWELLPRODUCTIONS.COM
Websites	WWW.SELFPUBLISHERSGROUP.COM
	WWW.INKWELLPRODUCTIONS.COM

Contact above address to order, or call/fax/e-mail for more information about this book or any book published by Inkwell Productions.

Credits

Edited by:	Patricia Turpin
Typesetting/design/layout by:	Madalyn Johnson
Cover Design by:	Paul Klissas
Cover Photograph:	Pat Warwick

Acknowledgements: A great thanks to His Holiness the Dalai Lama, Ven. Za Choeje Rinpoche, Oprah, Nick, Paul, Patricia, Sophia, the wonderful members of the Self Publishers Group, Cloe, Luise, Mike & Donna, Mark, Stuart, Brandon, Nelson, Pat, Copé, Bryan & Karen, Eric, Dan, Dave, Doug, The Gentlemen of the Regimental Band, General Sanelli, Hal, The Walbridge's, Danny & Mary Alice, The Hanley's, The Bosque Family, The Munizza's, The Gonzales's, The McDonough's, The Flood's, The Ambrose's, Rebecca, Patti, Maera, Towe, Rick, Francisco, Chris W, Rabbi Matt, Annie, Manuel, Ann, KC, Alyssa, Heidi, Billy, Mark, Yochanan, Renee, Suzanne, Mike R, Grandma Genie, Richard, Len, Don, The PARC staff, Wendy, Scott, Brother Jack, Vince, Brother Dan, Jane, April, Deb, Krisanne, Suzi, the guys from 944, the UC RA's, The guys of ZX, Fox Chase Cancer Center, Susan & the staff of hospice, Amy, Paul, Harry, Bonnie, Chris, The Wirth's, The Riley's, Dave G, the Spirit and staff of Hawk Mountain, John R, Pat, Shawn, Julie & Lucas, Sam, Beth & Isabelle, Casey, Angel & Ashley, Josef, Nate, Tricia, Brian, Brian, Ana, Nicole, Jocelyn, all of my friends everywhere, everyone I missed, the living Masters of our time (here & there), and Everyone and Everything that has, is, and will teach us about the beauty and magic of Love. I Love you all. Peace.

Eternally,

PRINTED IN THE UNITED STATES OF AMERICA

Honor to you

Great warriors of Love,

Mighty soldiers of Peace,

Past,

Present,

Future.

Thank you.

In your name

We live to Play

Another Day.

GAMEMASTER

Index

Reality : Gamemaster Manual

FOREWORD

My name is Robert Jacoby. I am the son of a Holocaust concentration camp survivor. That war is not yet over. In fact, there is a piece of the battlefield in each of us today. This conflict is waged against the obstructions to happiness, peace, meaning, and most of all Love. I, along with many others, am fighting that war.

My father is my first hero. Born Henry Jakubowitz, he was ripped from his home at a very young age, labored through five work camps, and found the resolve to keep living. As his family, friends, and loved ones perished by ways of terror and torture, my Father was spared. Each day he struggled to overcome his situation and survive. Despite innumerable odds, he fought to hold on. If he were alive today, he would say he survived for hope; that he had no choice but to keep on going. I know he survived for Love.

I believe that Love is the answer, the question, *and* the mystery. Amazing how a simple four-letter word is the basis for everything we do. Everything. Yet, we scoff at its presence, fear its wrath, and even kill to stop its fruiting. Without Love, life would be a painful journey toward nowhere. Love is not just another emotion in the game of life – it is the game.

I believe that Love takes many forms. Attraction, passion, and desire are only a few of the creative manifestations of Love. Hate, anger, and prejudice are the destructive manifestations. Plain and simple, we each have the power to create Love, or destroy it. The time has now arrived to put down the countless deadly words and weapons we humans have created over the ages. Have we not already mastered the destruction of Love? The answer is yes. We are now ready to become experts in its creation.

My journey, passions, scientific and professional focuses, have all centered on the enlightenment of the human spirit: the amazing journey to the center of ourselves. Over the years I have come to realize that for people to become enlightened, they must know Love. It appears that in this dawn of revisiting holistic medicine and universal spirituality, we are once again discovering the incredible powers of this illusive emotion.

We have been fighting the war for Love since the dawn of time. I believe that we are once again winning.

Although our planet is in a time of unrest and great change, there is one fact that has, is, and will eternally remain constant: we are getting closer to understanding and living in Love – Love for one another, for this life, and most of all, ourselves.

Love. It is the universal true constant, and the state of being from which all of life stems. It is about surrendering to the moment you are in, without reservation, and with open and innocent eyes. It is the nature of the soul. Experiencing life in this state of being does exist. There is a way to return to this place. A map back home.

I have been sharing the information in these pages with many people for many years in my roles as teacher, counselor, friend, and passing stranger. I have been blessed with the opportunity to watch those who remember Love, wake up, and begin again to believe in the magic of life. These people are winning the battle, and the flags of victory are marked by the smiles on their faces. Now *you* are the next person to remember the game of Love.

What you are about to read is a true story. I have kept most of it secret for years. I am now ready to share all of it with you. It's time.

Within these pages are the blueprints for life, the recipe for spontaneous healing, and the directions through the time-space continuum. These are the instructions back to the center of your being: the return to your soul.

Between these covers is a story about uncovering the *reality* we all share. Even more amazing, it is a story about YOU! Impossible, you say? Wonderful! You shouldn't believe everything your hear. However, nothing is impossible. And yes, this book is really about you.

Between these covers lie keys to unlock *reality*. Not just the reality that exists in each of us, but the *real reality*. The *reality* we are all part of. The place where you and I are one, without walls, deceit, or judgment. *Where the fun is!* Once these keys are used, there is no turning back. Ever.

You are about to begin your life over *again*. Fear may cause you to question what you are about to begin. You may wonder if you will ever be able to stop the process.

Have courage. You are about to uncover the truth about you, everyone, and everything. Once you begin this journey, you will not *want* to return. The nature of the spirit is such that it moves from struggle to happiness, dark to light, and pain to Love. You cannot escape your spirit; you cannot escape Love.

I am an ordinary man, but one on a relentless search for the meaning of it all. In that search, I have found a few keys to unlocking the truth of our selves as well as unlocking the questions that hide in the abyss of our souls. Did I find these answers? No. They found me. And now, they have found you. In fact, the answers in this book have been looking for you all of your life. They are looking for all of us. Your reading this book means they have found you once again.

Is there anything in this book you don't already know? Of course not. You have always known it. And just in case you forgot, *you know* ***everything***. This book is just another reminder of what you already know.

Many of us fall asleep and forget.

You are about to wake up
and remember.

CHAPTER 1 PROMOTION

> *"The real voyage of discovery consists*
> *not in seeking new landscapes,*
> *but in having new eyes"*
> *- Marcel Proust*

It was 10:00 a.m. on a Wednesday when my boss called me into his office. I could tell something was very wrong. I pulled his door shut and looked around at the somber faces of the rest of the hospital administration staff. The director told us that four employees had just quit, and we would need to cover their positions. At first, I was relieved. Filling in for other staff was just part of the job. No problem.

I had been counseling teenagers and addicts for a few years and thought, "It shouldn't be that difficult; at least it's something different, right?" That was until he told me that I would take over the ever-feared corrections unit. I would be counseling convicts and their families. I was driving right out of my comfort zone into a minefield.

Before that day, my job was pretty simple. I evaluated teenagers that parents, police, or probation officers dropped off at our door. I worked in a semi-locked drug rehab hospital. This was the last stop for most of our patients – last stop meaning that the next place they would go if they didn't clean up their acts was behind bars or below ground. These kids were not just going through problems or hooked on drugs, they were on the front lines of life and death. For a few minutes to a few months, they had been rescued from the battle; we hoped we could teach them to use the tools that would help them win the war.

These kids had been through the most challenging and terrifying of *Reality's* obstacles: abuse, abandonment, rejection, and fear. They had had enough of the game. They were done.

For every admission there was a story. An amazing story – one of hardship, struggle, and perseverance. Sure, they were now in rehab, but to hear of the events which had led each soul to this place of healing was enough to make anyone shudder. They were warriors, but they had given up.

After a few weeks, my fear of the boys in this all-male corrections unit had subsided. I had earned some respect by standing my ground the day they all rioted and escaped from the facility, but that's another story. It took me some time to get comfortable with the knowledge that at any second I could be attacked or killed. But at this point, fear wasn't an option. I had a job to do.

Almost daily as I was conducting therapy, I'd be interrupted by the sight of a swarm of staff members carting a screaming patient by my office on the way to the restraint and seclusion room. Once there, he or she would be strapped down, stripped of sharp objects, and given a tranquilizer. After a while, such sights were just part of the scenery. Rehab was an experience in surrealism.

One morning there was a staff meeting about one our residential patients. The staff needed to decide if one of the male teens should be transferred to corrections – to program with "the boys" as I called them. A great lesson was about to unfold.

Phoenix was a sarcastic felon on adult probation, and now in drug rehab. He had a long history of placements, as well as a lengthy criminal record. About 17 years old, he was at the final gate between himself and a long stay in prison. A devout white power fanatic, Phoenix was at first glance a scary person. Ironically, Phoenix couldn't understand why his peers didn't tolerate him. Even in prison and rehab there is a code of respect. Phoenix wasn't part of that code.

The hospital population was eighty to ninety percent Hispanic, Native American, and African American adolescents. Roughly ten to twenty percent were Caucasian. Phoenix let everyone know he considered himself to be "white." There just wasn't enough room for Phoenix.

With his aggressive behaviors and criminal history, Phoenix qualified to be transferred over to the correctional unit. The problem was that during the few weeks he spent on the residential side, Phoenix had made it a practice to throw up gang signs at "the boys," and started an all out war. They wanted his blood and they were about to get their chance.

Phoenix packed his things and moved into corrections room 12. His roommates were three hard-core gang members: two African American G's from the south side, and one Hispanic gangster who had

Brown Pride tattooed in five inch Olde English lettering across his back. All of them were more than happy to greet their new roomie. For weeks, Phoenix had made his bed – out of razor-sharp rusty nails – and now he had to sleep in it.

As I escorted him to my office, Phoenix stopped me and said, "You know that I'm dead over here, don't you? They've been gunning for me for weeks."

"Funny how that works, huh?" I said.

"What does that mean," snarled our new guest.

"Karma," I laughed, "Karma."

Earlier that morning I had had a group session with the boys about the negative consequences of feeding prejudice and hate. I wanted to soften the transition and hoped to prevent Phoenix from getting jumped that night. Getting jumped happened often, and sometimes it landed the victim in the hospital.

"They can go to hell. I'll kill all of them!" screamed Phoenix, as we discussed the trouble he had stirred up over the last few weeks.

"OK, but tell me how you really feel," I replied with a grim smile.

I always welcomed the expression of emotions – however negative. Getting feelings out is important. Even the ugly ones. However, it was obvious that Phoenix and I were way past the "let's get in touch with our feelings" stage.

He listed every minority group he hated, and the reasons for his stifling anger. I couldn't convince him that he had no real justification for his beliefs. His way was the truth, as it is with everyone. We each decide our own truth. Phoenix's "truth," however, was about to get him killed.

Phoenix wasn't the only one with a skewed version of the truth. In fact, all of the boys had distorted perceptions of *reality*. They weren't criminals for nothing – they were criminals for *something*, and proud of it. They considered themselves warriors of their lands – the enforcers of justice, the kings of their hills.

Once strapped with guns, and armed with a purpose, these chosen few were forced out of battle, and provided with another gift – one last chance at joining a truly meaningful struggle. This would be a tough transition for all of them to make, because on the home front, their battles still raged on. Whether they fought for pride, territory, drugs, or to escape the shackles of physical, sexual, and emotional abuse, they were all warriors anxious to return to battle.

But they were also tired. They were exhausted creations of their past. It was time to try and convince these boys of a different, more peaceful way to win their wars. Time was quickly running out – not just for Phoenix or the boys, but for all of us.

CHAPTER 2 INVITATION

"Things don't change. You change your way of looking, that's all."
-Carlos Castaneda

The boys were a little different from the other patients at the hospital. They had all come from a long history of failed therapy, countless psychotropic medications, and numerous correctional institutions. They ended up here because of their resistance to healing, and because someone believed that they could still be helped.

Convicts can see right through you. They have experienced so much deceit, abuse, and pain, that they recognize it from miles away. I had to be completely and utterly real with the boys. If I wasn't, they would know, and I would be written off as just another illusion in their drama. Being real and honest wasn't just their challenge, it was mine as well.

After a few weeks of running the program, I began to believe that maybe I had nothing to offer these guys. What more could I possibly say to help them wake up and realize the power they had over their lives? I understood that everything happens for a reason, but this situation made no sense to me. I had spent the last few years trying to help people who could grasp concepts like being at peace, and cultivating balance and harmony. The boys didn't know how to act from one minute to the next, let alone understand the value of stillness.

I usually went by the book when it came to counseling. Most of the counseling theories worked on just about everyone. But with the boys, conventional therapy obviously hadn't made a dent. This captive audience was not easily convinced about anything. Especially Love.

These warriors were lost, and needed the map back home. Lucky for them, a few years ago, during the expanse of an endless night, I found a copy. Or I should say, a copy found me.

Fear set in. Not the fear of being surrounded by dangerous

convicted felons. Fear of revisiting that night six years ago. A night that had followed me across time and space, through the desert, and back into my life.

I thought that I had left behind the adventure of that fateful night long ago. I was mistaken. Because Bubba, and the boys, reminded me that that night wasn't quite over. In fact, it had just begun.

I met Bubba a few months after I started working at the hospital. He was an interesting one. Towering at almost six and a half feet tall, bald, and armed with a drill at his side, Bubba was the last person you would want to run into in some back alley. At first glance, Bubba was just as intimidating as some of the boys. That is, until he started talking.

Out of the mouth of this mammoth person came the most gentle tones and kindest of words. He posed as the maintenance man, however, he would end up counseling the kids as they helped him patch up the facility. None of them even knew they were being schooled by Bubba. His wisdom was delivered between the patching of walls and painting of rooms. Bubba knew what he was doing, and he was doing it very well.

Bubba had been in rehab a few times himself. He spoke from experience. He had been through some hard times, and now lived with the hope to help even one kid.

One morning over a cup of coffee, we started talking. Bubba and I found we had many things in common. Bubba also played the didgeridoo, wrote poetry, practiced meditation, and was the outdoorsy type. Along with a slew of other shared interests, Bubba was also out to save the world. Meeting Bubba was not just a coincidence, it was fate. It's all fate.

As we got to know each other, we moved from discussing hiking trails to pontificating about spirituality and the nature of the cosmos. I felt comfortable talking with Bubba about my take on things – something I rarely do. I am glad I did, because thanks to Bubba, *The Manual* and I were reintroduced back into *The Game*. What is *The Manual* and *The Game?* I'll explain that later.

One afternoon, Bubba, and his friend Matt, who also worked at the hospital, invited me to take part in a sweat lodge ceremony with some of their friends on the reservation outside of town. This was the opportunity of a lifetime. I had spent most of my adult life studying about the many religions and beliefs of the world, and one of my dreams was to experience the healing traditions of the true natives of this country. I had always been fascinated by the wisdom of the original inhabitants of this planet. The Native Americans were at the top of my list. I was now invited to participate in one of their most sacred ceremonies. I was truly honored.

It was a warm and calm Sunday evening as I approached the reservation of the Salt River Pima Maricopa Indian Community. As I drove North on the 101, the vast desert landscape grew mystical before my eyes. The setting sky was painted a majestic orange, set artfully ablaze by nature herself. I was awestruck as I watched kaleidoscopic colors float across the backdrop of scattered clouds and the surrender of the sun at the horizon. I took the glory of the sky as a special sign. At the time I didn't realize that it was signaling the beginning of an end – an end to what remained of the reality I had spent years safeguarding, the end to ignoring the truth – and the beginning of my own sweet surrender.

I pulled off the highway and drove toward the reservation. Now on sacred land, I could hear the sound of drumming as I pulled onto the property. I grabbed my didge, and headed toward the flames of the bonfire where the others were gathered. As I approached the fire, I saw six men, standing entranced, drumming to the dance of the rising embers.

As the last of the sun's rays disappeared into the Arizona sky, it was time. The music ended. We smudged ourselves with desert sage, thanked our grandfathers, and entered the sweat. We were ready for the ascent into ourselves.

CHAPTER 3 LETTING ME KNOW

"Birth is not one act; it is a process.
The aim of life is to be fully born, though its tragedy is that most of us die before we are thus born. To live is to be born every minute. Death occurs when birth stops. Physiologically our cellular system is in a process of continual birth; psychologically, however, most of us cease to be born at a certain point."
-Eric Fromm

The sweat lodge ceremony takes place in a small dome tent, or teepee, typically framed with willow branches and covered in skin or wood. There is one opening into the dome, and a pit in the center for the heated, porous rocks. The sweat symbolizes the journey of life. You go in, sweat a little, sing a little, find yourself, and then come out.

The sweat consisted of four rounds, or sections. Each round was dedicated to one of the four directions. Each round had its own significance and purpose.

We entered, took our seats, and the ceremony began. Matt brought in the porous rocks, which had been baking in the bonfire all day long. He gathered two to three rocks at a time with a rake, and carefully placed them in the pit at the center of the dome. As each stone entered the dome, the heat rose exponentially. Francis, whose property we were on, started the chanting. As each prayer was sung, he would splash water over the porous rocks; the resulting steam spiked through each of us, bringing on the sweat. This continued on for more than four hours.

I was told that during the sweat you are cleansing your soul, mind, and body. You are also healing the past, present, and future. I agree. In the sweat you return to your true self – sometimes just by being, and sometimes through visions about your path.

As the night continued, I searched to understand the meaning behind the recent events of my life. How did I end up here? How did *The Manual,* my new responsibilities at work, and this ceremony all fit together? I could see that they were all signs of healing, but I wondered how it all fit together, as everything always does.

That's how I felt at the start of the final round. Halfway into the fourth round, amidst the heat and cedar smoke, I not only began to see how it all fit together, but how each piece was utterly crucial to all of the other pieces. The rumors about the sweat were true. A weight had been lifted. I felt I could breathe again.

As I drove to work Monday morning, I had changed. I was no longer carrying the fear I had harbored for years. I was at peace with who I was and what I had to say; therapy was about to look a little different.

First thing that morning, over our ritual cup of java, I thanked Bubba for an incredible experience. He was glad that I had had a good time, and asked how the evening affected me.

"I think I found something I had lost," I replied.

I asked Bubba to help me gather the boys in the group room. We were about to introduce a new game plan.

"Gentleman, I have heard your stories. I have seen the way each of you plays your game, from the way you manipulate others, to the cons you pull. Your games are very impressive. In fact, genius. Brilliant. You criminals have been convinced that you are stupid, and cannot amount to anything. Not true. The games you play in your lives take extreme intelligence, courage, and stamina. You are doing great using your minds!" At this point the staff, as well as the patients, were looking at me as if I had lost my mind. I had, but I also had their attention.

"You all have a way to play the game of life, and yet none of you are winning. You want power, wealth, respect, and excitement, yet time and time again you end up with misery, boredom, and pain. You hurt others trying to find beauty in life, and that beauty is already free for you to embrace. And still, time and time again, you cannot find the beauty in your own lives. None of you are playing life on life's terms. You have created your own games and play according to your own rules. Some of you cheat at life, some pretend, and others just quit. But all of you, as different as you may believe you are, are identical in three ways: first, each of you plays your own version of the game of life. Second, all of you are addicted to escaping reality whenever you can. Third, *you are all losing.*

"You are not addicted to the rush of your game, or to the high of the drugs. Not at all. No, no. All of you are doing whatever you can to hide from the world you live in. You are all cowards, afraid to wrestle with life as it is unfolding. Now, today, you have a choice. You either learn to play the game differently, or make room for someone who will! Now gentlemen, you're either in or you're out."

"OUT?! What do ya mean by that? What, leave?" barked Tyree, the hardest of the boys. "If we do that, then we go right back to jail!"

"Correct. See Tyree, you're a genius. It's simple. All of you have seconds left in the game of life, and there are those here who, though they won't admit it now because they are surrounded by a bunch of criminals, desperately need to learn the rules, and fast. But, if you're not ready to learn, you will only distract those who are. Remember boys, your future depends on you, and the future is almost here."

I was done. I had said what was in my heart, and it felt good. After a long silence, I asked, "So...who's in?" From twelve patients, rose twelve hands. The adventure was about to begin. The boys were ready to learn how to *win the game.*

Everyday, the boys, Bubba, and I practiced the art of nothing, letting go, and mastering the Gamemaster Manual. As the days passed, transformations occurred. We were all changing, including Phoenix, and it was amazing!

Each week we would practice meditation, mindfulness, and the art of being. When we were not sitting still, we traversed the trails of the fabled Superstition Mountains, learned to temper judgment, and just had fun.

Watching 12 of the scariest criminals you could ever imagine meditate for an hour, say thanks, and ask for more, was one of the most awesome things I have ever experienced. They were doing something few thought was possible – they were learning to Love themselves. They were becoming Masters.

The boys became the pride of the hospital, as well as themselves. They quickly cultivated manners, awareness, and a sense of happiness that radiated to everyone around them. Sometimes they would stumble and fall, but at least now they knew how to get up on their own and dust themselves off. Within a few short weeks, the boys became experts in the art of "excuse me," and "I'm sorry."

One late afternoon, a few weeks into our adventure, Phoenix knocked on my door with a perplexed look, and asked if he could talk to me. He sat down in a chair, put his head in his hands, and solemnly said, "I realize what kind of person I have been these past few years: a complete and total racist! Why did you even try with me? What made you care?"

I smiled at Phoenix and said, "We all deserve a second chance, and when that's gone, we have to work hard in order to earn the third, fourth, and fifth ones. You earned yours. You're still trying, and trying is the key."

I shared with Phoenix how judgment and prejudice had affected my own life. He began to see that not only were these his battles, they were mine as well. We were all in the battle, fighting the same enemy. As he looked at me questioningly, I passed onto him the stories my father told me about the concentration camps during World War II, describing the atrocities and horrors created by separation and judgment. I also told him stories of courage and heroism that were born out of the ashes of war by those who suffered at the hands of hate. Phoenix wanted to know more. We talked for hours on the subject, and as night approached, it was time to call it a day.

"One last question?" Phoenix said with his smug look, "So...why didn't you hate me from the beginning, knowing that I was prejudiced toward your background?"

"Well, why did you believe some stranger that you didn't even know could possibly help you?"

Phoenix paused, scratched his head, and politely said, "I guess I just took a chance."

"So did I."

Two years after our journey together, I ran into three of the original twelve boys from rehab. They were all doing well and told me that the reports of the other nine were also good. As for Phoenix, he now has an African American roommate, a steady job, and spends his time staying out of serious trouble.

If any one of you guys is reading this book, I want to thank you. You helped me realize that we cannot hide from who we are. Ever. You taught me that everyone has the ability to heal and change, and that there is Love in all of our hearts.

Even more importantly, you proved to me that everyone can become a Gamemaster.

CHAPTER 4 STAGE ONE

"Nirvana may be the final object of attainment, but at the moment, it is difficult to reach. Thus the practical and realistic aim is compassion, a warm heart, serving other people, helping others, respecting others, being less selfish."
-H.H. Dalai Lama

Well, I see that this book has found you. You must be looking for something. Well, aren't you? Most of us are. The amazing thing is that most of us don't even know what that somethingoranother is. We just know that we are looking for it, and hope that it will all make sense when we find it.

This book finding you is no accident. There are no accidents in the universe. None. Accidents just don't happen.

At this very second, it may appear that we are abandoned on a very large floating ball, spinning in the middle of something we call deep space for absolutely no reason whatsoever. We have no idea where we really are, where we came from, or what is really going on here. What we do know, however, is that we are trying our best to make sense of it all, and have a good time while we're doing it.

If you are one of the ones on this planet who is not having a good time, then *WAKE UP!* You could be gone at any second. Time is precious, and meant to be enjoyed.

It's all just a matter of time.

Wouldn't you want to be having a blast with your last few seconds of living? If you answered 'yes,' then this book is for you. And if you are one of the lucky ones who is currently having a good time, well, this book is for you, too! You can never have too much fun.

So…are you *really* ready?? Maybe so, but you don't have to answer that question just yet. There will be a point later in this book, or long after you place it on your shelf, that the question of readiness will reappear: you will then have to ask yourself if you are once again ready to cross the bridge.

Crossing this bridge connects us to the truth. That moment is different for each of us. But make no mistake, there is a bridge, and at some point you will need to cross it.

This bridge connects our inner and outer lives. It is the bridge to our souls and true identities. Our souls being the true constants in the ever-changing universe. We cross it when we are ready to let go of our preconceived notions about the way things should be, and yield to see what actually is.

Allow me to offer a word of caution. If you do decide to venture to the other shore, you will never be able to turn back. Nothing in your reality will ever be the same again. But don't worry, that's not a bad thing. As for turning around and going back, you won't want to. Would you choose stale bread when you can have fresh croissants?

If you do decide to turn around halfway across the bridge, you can. Most do. The *truth* can be a little much. In that case, this book will merely reside as fiction in the caverns of your mind, but the opportunity to cross the bridge will continue to present itself time and time again. Unless you are truly ready, you will not cross the bridge.

If you are ready, and decide to cross, you will embark on a journey beyond your wildest dreams. Maybe this is just a dream? Well then, better finish reading before you wake up. You don't want to spend the whole dream reading about dreaming, now do you?

Who are we? Why do we exist? What happens after the game is over? What the heck is really going on here! The answer: you. You are going on here. Without you, there is no *reality*. Is a picture a picture, if no one is there to look at it? Would all of this be happening if you weren't here to see it? Doesn't life feel like it is a movie about you, and everyone you meet is part of the script? Of course it does, and you are the starring role. The hero of this game. *The master of your universe.*

You are creating your reality. Right this second. Isn't it you that chose to read this far?

What is *The Game* you ask? You're playing it right now. Yes, this very second! We are all playing *Reality: The Game of Lifetimes,* but most of the world doesn't even know it *yet*. They're sleepwalking through it. Much like playing a video game with your eyes closed, and expecting to win. That's not fun or very effective, now is it?

Each one of us is right in the middle of an awesome intergalactic adventure. However, only some of us realize it. This adventure is about many things: the celebration of who we are, the exploration of why we are here, and mastering the creation of *Love*.

Some call *The Game* life, reality, earth, heaven, hell, or the hokey pokey. Whatever you want to call it is fine, but remember, we are all playing the same game, with the same name, in the middle of the same place.

Isn't it about time we all read the same directions, and got on the same page?

The time has come to put down the pain, and enjoy our moments together, as one. That is the game of Love, and you are about to become an expert in it. So, assuming you really are playing a game in the middle of the universe, and you really are the hero, you'll need to know what's really going on and how to win.

You will need to become

A

GAMEMASTER.

CHAPTER 5 FIXATION

"Meditation is not about some state, but about the meditator. It's not about some activity, or about fixing something, or accomplishing something. It's about ourselves."

-Charlotte Joko Beck

Quickly shaking my head back and forth, I prayed that it would be over and time would start up again. "What am I saying?" I thought. "My God, what happened? What have I done?"

Only moments ago everything around me had stopped; everything. I had left time behind. I was somewhere else. I couldn't believe what I had just experienced. "I've really done it now!" I thought to myself. For the first time in my entire life, I felt that I had gone way too far. I had definitely crossed over something, and no matter how prepared I thought I was to cross, I was dead wrong.

Funny, because for a brief while, I just thought that I was dead. And this was only the beginning.

I wanted to regain my composure and quickly piece together what I used to think was reality. I will never be able to completely describe what I experienced that evening. There are not enough words in all of our known languages to convey the objective and subjective details of that night.

It was like skydiving, or falling in Love. If you've done it, no one needs to tell you how it feels. If you haven't, no one can ever convey to you what it's like. To understand it, you'll just have to experience it for yourself.

I had traveled to another place, hidden within this world and our visible reality. And as much as I was thrown by the whole experience, it didn't feel that strange at all. It was what I had been searching for all my life. It was what I wished for.

I want you to know that I am as scientific as I am spiritual. A few years ago if you had told me what I am telling you now, I would have written you off as having watched too many late night Twilight Zone episodes. I was a solid non-believer. Was.

What I experienced that night wasn't an illusion. It was real, and it scared the death right out of me!

Coming out of the meditative state I was rattled – shaking uncontrollably, terrified, and speechless. Utterly speechless. Later as I learned about mystical and near-death experiences, I found that this reaction was normal and to be expected.

I had been practicing meditation for a while, but until this experience, I did not grasp its full power or potential. Most people think that sitting still and breathing is an uneventful hobby practiced by tree huggers and yogis with nothing to do on a Saturday night. That's what *I used to think*. I was wrong.

I have done my fair share of exploring non-ordinary states of consciousness and rummaging through the basement of the mind, but only one thing could have prepared me for what I saw that night, and that was everything. Everything I had ever experienced helped prepare me for that evening; however, even my everything wasn't enough to prepare me for the transformation that was now beginning to take place.

We all change. Each nanosecond we are exploding with new life. Our physical, spiritual, mental, and emotional bodies are growing at light speed. We just don't realize it because we are used to ourselves. Look at how fast a child grows. This does not slow as you get older. It speeds up.

Over the span of our lives we notice these changes to some degree. Changes in appearance, mindset and emotional triggers are only some of the ways we can tell we're evolving. This meditation experience was part of the evolution of my soul, but instead of baby steps, I had taken a quantum leap.

The term "mystical experience" took on a new meaning for me, and everything changed: my somewhat simple life, my perception of the truth, and what I once called reality. What used to be real was now *real* different, and so was I. I had lost my reality, and it didn't look like I was going to get it back anytime soon. When you question what "real" is, the questions are only beginning.

The adventure I had been searching for was now real. The game was on. There was no turning back. I had crossed the bridge I had been searching for all along, but also came back with more than I bargained for. Across the bounds of time and space, I had returned with the location of the bridge, and the directions on how to get back – the *Gamemaster Manual*.

My first questions were "who else knows about this place, this state of mind? Who else understands the *truth* about Love?" I thought about great figures of our time, and realized that many have traveled there: Ghandi, Buddha, Mother Theresa, Jesus, Lennon, Dave Matthews, Sara McLachlan, and many more. The list just goes on. Our greatest teachers had been to this place, and had dedicated their lives to teaching others about the peace we can have in this world. They were the Gamemasters, and their teachings were from the manual as well.

There are many Masters among us today. They, too, are teaching from the *Gamemaster Manual*. Some paint, some sing, some dance, and some act. Each Master teaches in her or his own way, but the message is the same: each of us has an infinite and eternal source of power, a jewel, buried in the rubble of our lives. It is hidden in the depths of our souls. It can be found, and when you find it, your life embodies the magic and beauty it was meant to have.

You return to Love.

So what was it I experienced that night? Love. Absolute Love.

Dream of a place away from time, the most beautiful landscape your mind can possibly create. Now spruce it up a bit more. Imagine that this place shines with pure Love, peace, and joy. You feel it wherever you are. You can't escape the happiness. Now imagine that everyone you ever knew and didn't know was there. Add music, laughter, and another dash of Love, and you still haven't come close to the realities of *reality*.

I have seen enough in this world to know what is real and what isn't. This was real, and it changed my life permanently. It is now *my reality*. It is alive in my everyday. The biggest thing I realized that night was that we are not searching for answers about ourselves, life, Love and God. It's just the opposite. The answers are looking for us. We just need to stand still long enough to hear what they have to say. And when we stop to listen, we as a family will never be the same.

As we begin to understand the nature of ourselves, it is then that we are able to see the beauty and reason behind life. As human beings, we are about to start playing the game the way it was meant to be played. With Love. And *that* is beautiful.

Was it real? Some would say it wasn't, others would say it sounds great for a book. Well, it does. But it was real, and still is. It exists right now. *Reality* is going on all around us, and I didn't find it. It found me. And now, it has found you. Shortly, you will come to the foot of the bridge. You, too, will have to decide whether to cross. It's just a matter of time.

It's all just a matter of time.

CHAPTER 6 THE SEEDS OF PASSION

"There is no end. There is no beginning.
There is only the infinite passion of life."
-Federico Fellini

So how did this whole mess begin anyway? Some call it stubbornness, others call it curiosity. I call it just trying to get by. I have always been a seeker. A seeker of what you ask? The truth. The truth about you, me, and what's really going on here. My search began a long time ago, and after the night *The Manual* found me, I realized that my search had been going on far longer than I originally thought. That night changed me, everyone I have met, and ever will meet. That "everyone" now includes you, too.

As a child I spent my time trying to fly off the roof pretending to be a superhero, and in between jaunts around the block, I found my peace amidst the treetops in the back yard. It was among the branches of the tall oaks that I would stare at the clouds and stars as they danced across the heavens. I believed that I could recharge my superpowers in the trees, and maybe next time around, I might finally get off the ground. At the time I didn't realize that my desire to be among the peaceful inhabitants of the floating sky would be a recurring theme in my life.

I liked being way up in the trees. You could see everything from up there. Not only could I see my house, but everyone else's. At night I would lay in bed, wishing that I could find a tree big enough that I could see everything and everybody. How big was this place, and were there others who could fly high above the treetops?

Well, be careful what you wish for. With wishes, it's not a matter of "if" they happen, but "when" they happen. *It's just a matter of time.*

I grew up in a small town nestled in the Pennsylvania countryside, with my mom, dad, younger sister, and the occasional turtle or squirrel. My parents were Polish immigrants, and very much from the old world. My Father was a concentration camp survivor and my Mother the youngest daughter of a depression-era family.

When I was about seven years old, my Father asked if he could speak with me outside. I suspected that this meant I was in some kind of trouble. Usually I would have enough time to prepare myself for such a meeting by placing a book in my pants to protect my rear end, but this one took me off guard.

"Can I show you something?" he said. I thought for sure this was it.

Instead of a whooping, he led me into the crawlspace under the house. He told me how much he appreciated the fact that I was always curious about how things work, and my eager willingness to fix anything that broke. Then he opened the door to the crawlspace, and there it was: the graveyard of my curiosity. My mother's toaster, my sister's Easy Bake Oven, an old boom box, and more. Much more. There were dozens of electronics, appliances, and toys that I had dismantled over the years. Just sitting there. Lifeless.

My dad turned to me with a worn look, and pleaded, "Could you just wait until they're broke before you try to fix them?" And so I did. Patiently, I waited to hear some gadget or small appliance start clicking or clacking.

During our childhood, my sister and I were raised like kids in most somewhat normal families, until my parents decided to try on dysfunction. Some families try dysfunction for a few moments here and there. We tried it on and forgot to take it off.

I was surrounded with a great deal of pain and chaos for most of my adolescent years. Not just family chaos, but chaos in general. I guess that's just part of growing up. I was the kid under the black cloud. It was always raining, and my umbrella was always left at home.

My parents fought often, and bad. It was awful to see people, who are supposed to be loving, sweet, and supportive, beat the very Love that brought them together, out of each other. And the ones around them.

They had survived violence, a world war, poverty, and despair. The saddest thing is that neither of them knew how to keep the destructive energy of their pasts from invading the present moment. Their pain eventually entered into our lives.

Most people *re*-create their lives based on how they were created.

This isn't good, especially if what you were handed as a kid was pretty bad, but it's easy to do. We easily pass on bad habits unless we realize that they are just that: bad habits.

Then there are those who truly *create* their lives and the lives of others, by breaking free from past family patterns and legacies. Growing up in such a dysfunctional environment, I quickly learned what Love isn't, how not to treat others, and how not to be treated.

Their fighting seemed to last forever. Finally the two of them grew so old and tired that they could not fight each other anymore. Later in my life I realized they were not even fighting each other; they were fighting themselves. We all do this – fight with everyone around us, ignoring the stark reality that *we are actually fighting a part of ourselves.*

My sister and I learned many lessons from the family drama. If you asked us if we would do it differently, we would say absolutely not. Neither of us would have changed it for anything. It has helped us become who we are, and has taught us about who we want to be. As we grew more conscious and aware of our lives, we realized that our parents had done the best they could, with what they had, at the time that they had it.

Growing up we didn't know of anyone else's parents who acted like ours, and thought it must be because they were Polish. It wasn't until several years later that we realized what we were experiencing was not just happening in our home, or because our parents were from "somewhere else," it was going on in a lot of other homes as well. Turns out almost everyone harbors some sort of secret.

Oftentimes people don't ask for help because they think their experience is so painful and unique that no one else will be able to understand it. The truth is that many others are facing similar pains at this very moment. They, too, are keeping quiet.

Many generations have passed before us and traveled down the trails of existence. We are not, and never will be, the only ones to struggle. This is something that we as humans have in common. No one gets through the game unscathed. The radiant beauty of diamonds is created under extreme pressure. Humans are no different.

Eventually my sister and I made a break to find out who we were. I headed off to college, and a few years later, my sister joined the military. As I entered my first year of undergraduate studies, I began to hear myself again. As the craziness around me subsided, I felt a tugging on my mind. Something was calling me.

CHAPTER 7 THE VESPERS OF ILLUMINATION

"The quieter you become, the more you can hear."
- Baba Ram Dass

I stood motionless on the parade field the first day at the academy. Here, in this spot, stood some of the greatest leaders of our time. This was going to be the experience of a lifetime. But not everybody would see it that way. The Rock, like all of life, was a test of perspective. Most would graduate, some would fail, and the rest would just pack up and take off. Only a few would uncover the truth, and *The Game*.

In general, only three types of individuals end up at a military academy. The first are slaves to the juvenile justice system, the second are those who want to be groomed for the military ideal, and the third are those who took a wrong turn on the way to Wonderland. I guess that I was a combination of all three.

I ended up at the academy following a dream. My goal in life was to be a fighter pilot. I thought the academy was the way to achieve my passions. It was. However, my true passion had yet to be revealed.

The Rock, like any military school, was based on a system of action and consequence. Every action, positive or negative, resulted in almost immediate praise or punishment. You do well, you get ahead. If you screwed up, you were cleaning statues and toilets with a toothbrush for three days.

I set my alarm early that first morning; I was determined to play and win this game. I had years of experience running around the Pennsylvania Appalachian Mountains with their cadet search and rescue programs. Over those years I had cultivated a solid background in military protocol. As a high school student, my weekends were filled with rock climbing and grueling wilderness survival training. I figured I could conquer this playing field, too.

"REVILLE! REVILLE!" yelled the bugler at the end of the hallway. "OUT OF YOUR RACKS AND IN THE CORRIDOR," screamed the officer in charge as he kicked in our door. A look between confusion and frustration took over his face as he saw that my roommates and I had risen early to get a jump on the game, and his scare tactic didn't work. Getting one up on the staff was only part of the fun here.

There was a lot to get used to at the academy. Up at 0450 hours, physical training at 0515, breakfast at 0545, band rehearsal at 0600, back to the barracks, clean up, and ready for the day by 0745. And that was only the morning.

I quickly became accustomed to the lime green corridors that reeked of floor polish, brass cleaner and patent leather shoes, and the sight of cadets filling those corridors, scurrying from one class to the next in full uniform. Often, it felt like I was in some kind of movie. Maybe I was.

The beginning of my tour at the academy involved "plebe training." I was now a member of the famous Regimental Band – the same band that had performed for countless dignitaries, ambassadors, and U.S. presidents for decades. We, the new cadets, were the "plebes." The initial training period focused on learning to play while marching, cleaning and polishing just about everything, and military courtesy and discipline. A couple of weeks into the year, academics were introduced to the already rigorous schedule.

Class was important, especially if you wanted to go off campus. Home meant my waterbed and beer. Class was now my number one priority.

My 7th period German class was taught by a short man with a head of tiny curls dressed in a neatly pressed military uniform. "Guten tag gentlemen, welcome to class."

At first, class with Colonel Weise was like any other class at the academy: one teacher and a few students plowing through text books at light speed. However, there were some days when the rest of the students were attending to other obligations, and it would be just the Colonel and I.

On these days, our conversations quickly transcended the class material, and turned to discussions about philosophy, psychology, and life in general. We talked about everything from meditation to reincarnation. This was the beginning of my awakening.

As I became more inquisitive about the Colonel's wisdom, he

suggested books like *Siddhartha, The Tao of Pooh,* and *The Greatest Miracle in the World.* Slowly, I was becoming conscious of the fact that life has many, many layers, and there are an infinite number of things going on around us all the time. Even more interesting, I learned that even though we all live here, on Earth, each of us is having a totally different adventure.

As I read the wisdom in these books, I couldn't wait to get back to class, hoping it was empty, to discuss my findings and ask more questions. As the year went on my thirst for this dialogue increased. I came to refer to my class with Colonel Weise as my philosophy lesson, my enlightenment, and the starting line to *The Game.*

Colonel Weise was a Gamemaster. He transcended all common categorizations of the human experience. He was a living Bodhisattva – a being who has returned to enlighten other masters – a Gamemaster on an intergalactic search and rescue mission.

It was at the academy that my suspicions of the bridge and other realities were confirmed. And the more I read, the more I realized the bridge did exist. I began to prepare for my walk across.

I realized that as we tell the universe who we want to become, it is already helping us get there. There is a catch. The end point will be your request, the path, however, will be up to *reality.* You will always get there, but never the way you thought you would. Be patient, you will always reach you in the end.

CHAPTER 8 EXODUS FROM THE CAVE

"Chaos demands to be recognized and experienced before letting itself be converted into a new order."
-Hermann Hesse

There was always a great deal of chaos at The Rock. From the cadences of marching cadets, to the carillon bells of the chapel, there was always something stirring at the academy. Throughout campus you could hear the Bandsmen of the Corps skillfully practicing their scales. Occasionally, you could hear the sweet serenade of *Amazing Grace* on the bagpipes weaving its way through towering pines and over the lush rolling green hills.

Behind the hussle and bussle of hectic cadet life was a world of sheer beauty and magic. The campus grounds were immaculately groomed. There were colorful, lively flowers surrounding every building, as well as the cannons and majestic statues which had guarded these fields for almost a century. You felt the magical spirit of this place everywhere you went.

Towards the end of the first semester a great pressure began to surface in my heart. I could literally feel something was happening to me, but for the life of me couldn't explain what it was.

Looking back, I can say it was like feeling my entire personality shedding off – like breaking out of a cocoon and taking my first flight. Most of us notice this metamorphosis at some point in our lives. It happens more often than you think. Some people feel it many times in their journey. Some never notice it at all.

This type of transformation happens when you start exploring your world, learning new things about it and yourself and asking why at every step, until you understand how and why you are making each step. As this happens, your mind and soul begin to create a chain reaction that shakes your perception of what is happening in *reality*. As this transformation continues, you are essentially getting a little closer to who you are, were, and always will be. The transformation is about getting back to you; now.

Months passed by. Each day I gazed out of the window in the Colonel's class and noticed the changing of the trees. On some level I believed that the trees and I walked together through the cycle of the seasons and of our fragile little lives. We moved from fall to winter. As winter was drawing to a close, the time to be reborn arrived. Spring was here, and I could feel that I was getting closer to something, or should I say it was getting closer to me.

As the year drew to a close, Colonel Weise no longer taught me anything I didn't already know and believe. He was now challenging me to uncover those things I had always known, but had covered up. I realized that I had painted over many facets of myself so that I could fit in and be accepted. Ironically, in order to be accepted by all, you must betray the one person most important to you: *yourself.*

The worst thing about covering up parts of yourself is that you forget where you came from and where you are going. Goals, wishes and dreams are created by the false you – the one you created to gain acceptance. For the first time in my life I was dreaming from a new center. Myself.

One part of me was now a dedicated follower in the system of the cadet corps, the other, some space ranger in search of the next shuttle back to home base. The universe has a sense of humor alright! Something was bound to give. *It was just a matter of time.*

Out of place, out of time, and out of my head – one day it all came to a screaming halt. I was leading two separate lives that were stretching in two different directions. The rubber band was ready to snap back.

One fine spring day as I marched back to the barracks from Colonel Weise's class, the change began to happen. I could literally feel my mind, nervous system, and perspective of *reality* shift. It was so sudden and intense that it scared the stripes right off my uniform pants. In an instant, I heard everything, clearly, without the noise of me. Dazed, I continued on down the walk to the upper parade field. The silence continued. Now standing on the pavement among the marching tours and drill practice, I began to accept what was happening. It was true. All of it. I experienced the human ability to transcend time, and to be completely at one with yourself and everything. It did and does exist, and it found me on my way back from class. My jaw dropped and I froze.

I had received an important clue. The proof of different layers of this world, the reality of peace and tranquility, and most of all – the reality of *reality*.

When the soul is searched for, and is done so relentlessly, it will awaken. When it does, you will know. Believe me. I had awakened something inside of me. I was turning into someone or something else. Actually, I was re-turning to wholeness. Back to myself. This was the first step in locating the bridge.

Now I understood what the Colonel was doing, and realized that he knew more than he ever claimed to know. In fact, he claimed to know nothing, and cited the books his information came from. In *reality,* in truth, whatever, he knew everything. That's because he had already accepted that he was part of everything.

He was the first Gamemaster I would meet in this round. He returned to show me, and others, the way out. Plato's *Allegory of the Cave* made complete sense. That day I learned that everything I had ever felt and believed was true. That was the mind-blowing experience of my soul's first awakening. At that instant, every aspect of fear, worry, and confusion died. I no longer needed them, and for now, they were gone.

After a few minutes the intensity of the experience subsided, but it wasn't over. I couldn't concentrate or sleep for days. During that time all I could do was try and grasp what was happening to me. The way I saw everything had been changed. My perspective included a new degree of clarity. There was more than just one world going on around me. There were universes upon universes upon universes.

What prevented this awakening from happening earlier in my life? I wasn't ready. It was fear and denial that kept me away from myself, and it is fear that keeps you away from yourself. All these years of listening to the messages from everyone but me went into the equation of denying true *reality*.

Every answer to every question was there. It always had been. And now it was all very, very real. Colonel Weise had gone down this road long ago, left the cave, and traveled across the bridge. He made it his work to return, and show others the way out. The real class was now in session.

In a second, my goals of manning fighter jets paled in comparison to transcending and understanding *reality* further. I felt like I needed to share this experience, as the Colonel had done with me, and help others to the foot of the bridge as well.

I decided to head in a different direction. My true passions were revealed, or should I say re-revealed. They never changed from my days as a child. I combined my Love for flying through the clouds, gazing at stars, and search and rescue, then plotted a new course.

This wasn't the bridge; however, it was the undeniable proof that it existed. A clue from *reality* that there was more. A roadsign leading to the foot of the bridge.

As the second year progressed, the Colonel and I continued our discussions, and I continued to grow. Cultivating peace, patience, and practicing standing still. Toward the middle of my sophomore year, I applied to local schools for a degree in psychology. I was only beginning to learn about *reality*. The second year came and went, and I prepared myself for yet another adventure.

CHAPTER 9 TIL TEARS DO US PART

"In the depths of winter, I finally learned that within me there lay an invincible summer."
- Albert Camus

I transferred my credits to a nearby coed college and began the remainder of my undergraduate career. The heart and soul were my new frontiers, and my goal was to become a counselor. I also exchanged my uniform and Sunday parades for blue jeans and house parties.

I didn't realize how great the difference was going to be between The Rock, and Caulfield College: better food, more freedom, and more fun. I spent as much time celebrating as I did studying. For the first time I understood why so many of my friends claimed that college is one of the best times of your life. It was, and still is.

I studied theory, practice, and science of the mind. There was so much information that sometimes it was hard to make it all fit together. Everyone seemed to have a take on the way things are, but most were not willing to consider the idea that maybe everybody was right. Everyone had a piece of the puzzle. It just needed to be put together.

Study by day – party by night. This was the steady rhythm of my academic career. As my senior year drew to a close, so did my celebration. At the end of spring break that year, my father called to tell me that he had not heard from my mother in over a week. Although irresponsible at times, she would usually call him to check in. As I talked with my dad, I was filled with a certainty that my mother was no longer in this world. I had prepared for, and dreaded, this moment for years.

I called her house, and after what seemed like endless ringing, a voice answered. It was a police officer who had just arrived. I asked him if she was still alive. He asked me if I could come to the house. I knew, and I cried.

My mother and I talked less and less after I left for college, mainly because I would not ignore her drinking and constant self-loathing. Each time she called, I would let her know how sad I was about her relentless self-destruction. I had exhausted every possible way of saying "Please, get it together."

In time, I became exhausted as well. She was determined to cash out. I was determined not to let her take me down, too. I felt I had one choice: I had to let her go. We stopped talking.

A visit to her house revealed that her soul had passed on a few days previous. Her decomposed body vaguely resembled the woman I once knew as my mother. The toxicology report showed that she had committed suicide with sedatives and vodka. She was tired of life, and had quit the game a long time ago. Only this time, she succeeded in creating the second portion of her roundtrip ticket.

One week after I had collected myself enough to return to school I received a call from my sister. She had returned from the army to attend our mother's funeral. This call was about my father: he was going into emergency surgery.

My father had fought with cancer since I was in high school, but it had been under control for the last few years. Now the cancer had spread. The surgery was to remove tumors near the arteries in his left leg. There were three possible outcomes: he would survive and the leg would be saved, he would survive and the leg would be amputated, or he would die.

The surgery was as much a success as it could have been. His leg was saved, however, while under the knife, the doctors found that the cancer had spread everywhere. His remaining time on Earth was limited to days.

I managed to get through the last few weeks of school and fumble through finals. Death was my new professor, and the true tests were being administered outside of the classroom. As I pulled away from the dorm on the last day of school, I stared at the graduation tassel dangling from my rearview mirror. I was looking back and driving forward. I knew that the days with my father were limited, and I didn't have time to grieve for my mother. Everything seemed to be spinning out of control.

In my mind, as I looked back at the road leading up to this point in my life, I could see the footsteps of the many people who accompanied me thus far on my path buried in the sand. As they got closer, I could see that one of them had faded out. Those steps were my mother's. As I looked on, I felt another set of prints beginning to fade. These were my father's. At many points along our journeys, new footsteps land, others return home. We must honor each step, for each step of each soul is sacred. I was determined to savor every last one of them.

At first I thought that these life events were a distraction from my quest to understand more about *reality,* and find the bridge. However, it didn't take me long to realize that these events were actually clues to the location of the bridge, and the most important lessons of life: Love, Love, and just when you think you're done – Love some more. We never know when it's the last time we'll be able to tell that someone we Love them.

It's all just a matter of time.

CHAPTER 10 AMAZING GRACE

"If there is to be any peace it will come through being, not having."

-Henry Miller

I was now more certain than ever that somewhere on the other side of the bridge was an antidote for the pain of grief. Isn't that what we are all looking for? An antidote for pain and suffering? Life would then be perfect. Isn't death what we're really scared of? Although I felt that I had come close to the bridge a few years ago, I realized I hadn't yet crossed it. There was more. At this point in the game my search for the bridge was no longer a casual interest, it was a necessity.

The greatest human fear is that we do not exist after death. We are afraid that it's over when it's over. The second greatest fear is, if it isn't over when it's over, what's next? When we come to this place of fear, we need an antidote.

Senior year came to a close, and I had been truly struggling with the challenge of living, knowing that death is about to knock on the door at any second, while enjoying time with my father as if nothing is going on. Now that's irony! Live each second like it is your last, but at the same time, live each second as if you're going to live forever. It was time to get to know who my dad really was. As I would learn about him, I would learn more about me.

My father's life was pretty simple his last days. I often wondered if he knew of his true nature, peace, and the bridge. Over the years I had only heard glimpses of his experience of this world, of life, and of God. He believed that when it's over, it's over. Done.

There are two common reactions among Holocaust survivors, war veterans, or anyone who experiences incredible pain: they become fully immersed in their faith in the universe, or denounce it altogether. Ever since I had known him, my father had chosen the latter.

Throughout my youth, I heard that my father believed in a God, but had no trust or faith in Her. He was raised Jewish, and my mother Catholic. When we attended church as kids, my father stayed home.

My father often raised the question that if there was a God, someone or something running the show, then why did he suffer through so much death and despair? How could a loving and omnipotent God allow such destruction to happen in *Reality?*

As the days passed, my father and I began to talk about things we had never discussed before: the passions of his youth, his experiences in the camps, and our relationship. He always had a difficult time showing love, and still did. He was funny that way. Neither of my parents really understood how to show Love to each other, or to their kids. We knew though. We felt it.

My father and I talked late into each evening. Each conversation was priceless and precious. I realized the gift that death delivered: the importance and fragility of now.

Just as I was getting to know my father better, the current of my life pulled me from his side. I received word that I had been accepted into grad school. It was time to move on. We had repaired our relationship, and I knew my father would be okay, and that when he did pass on, I would see him on the other side.

Preparing to go off to school I began to see that life doesn't stand still long enough to get a hold on it. That is just the way it is. In fact, life is never standing still, and you can never get hold of it. *It has hold of you.*

We believe that we are standing on the banks of the river of life watching it go by, but in *reality* we are in the water being towed by the current, watching the banks go by. Sometimes the current seems to be lifting us above the surface, and carrying us gently down the river's path. Other times it seems we have fallen into the raging trenches of a rapid's trap, our only recourse to take a last breath and surrender. Either way, *The Game* has you, and you're moving.

Now more than ever I felt a responsibility to help those still trapped in the cave, who could not see the bridge. I could not be selfish. I had to continue. Life was not about to ease up. It looked and felt like I was running away from fear; I knew I was running into it.

CHAPTER 11 TILT

"If a man should conquer in battle a thousand and a thousand more, and another man should conquer himself, his would be the greater victory, because the greatest of victories is the victory over oneself."

-The Dhammapada

As I began my master's degree, my world was collapsing. Trapped in the eye of the chaotic tornado, all I could do was watch it spin out of control. I was in a race against time, but aren't we all. That's what half of *The Game* is: time. To win, we must let go of the things that prevent us from winning the other half of *The Game:* Loving and being Loved at every moment.

You win when you allow yourself to feel the beauty of Love through every part of yourself and your soul at every second of every day. It is in the presence of Love that time stands still, and the tornado becomes a whisper: a sweet gentle whisper.

It takes the strength of a warrior just to live. We are challenged to live life as if pain and death do not exist. Even when pain and death are staring at you over breakfast, smoking a cigarette, and drinking a cup of coffee.

I moved into my own apartment, attended class, and bartended at the local coffee shop. I was living in a quaint, rustic town on the outskirts of Philadelphia. Resting along cobblestone streets, "the hill" was like a world of its own. Art galleries and antique shops lined the steep trolley path into the city, and it often seemed that no one in town worked. They just drank latte's, collected that day's paper, and hung out.

In between class and work, I began to practice meditation regularly. When I wasn't practicing meditation, I was studying its theoretical concepts. As I learned more about this timeless practice, I began to understand that it was not only a powerful tool to attain enlightenment, but to manage it as well.

Enlightenment happens in an instant. Poof! You're enlightened. Great! Congrats! A second later, you're not. Enlightenment isn't something that happens once and you're done. It is the constant practice of standing still, being, and Loving every second. Standing still, however, does take some work. Enlightenment is the gift that keeps on giving, as long as you are willing to keep unwrapping it.

On a cold December day at the coffee bar, one of our regular customers came in to get her vanilla soymilk steamer. It was right before the peak of the holiday season. The hillside was dusted with a layer of snow, and the trees were barren.

I liked getting to know the regulars that came into the store and made small talk with all of them. The sweet scent of incense preceded this woman as she came up to the bar. I gave her her drink, and wished her a great holiday.

She replied, "Thank you very much, but I do not celebrate these holidays."

I was curious as to what she did celebrate. Too often in life we are afraid to ask what others believe, and how they live their lives. Sometimes those very people have the next clue for you: everyone has pieces of the puzzle. Sometimes all you need to do is ask.

She said that she belonged to the Hare Krishna congregation down the street. It was one of the biggest centers on the East Coast. I told her about my fascination with world religions, and she invited me to stop by and visit.

I wanted to know more. I had learned of many beliefs over the years, and made it a practice to take part in the ceremonies and services of each to get a deeper understanding of their spirit – from Catholicism and Judaism as a child, to Buddhism, Taoism, Gnosticism, and many others in college. I heard what each one believed, but still did not *feel* any of them. Somehow, my understanding of these beliefs and my experience of life did not yet coincide.

I entered the center for The International Society for Krishna Consciousness, and the sweet smell of sandalwood and Nag Champa permeated the air. My friend from the coffee shop and her husband greeted me at the door. We sat down and discussed the tenants of their faith and their guidelines for living – what I call the way they play *The Game.*

To my surprise, it was similar to faiths I had come across. There was a code of kindness, a practice for stillness, and the belief that *The Game* goes on forever. The focus with the Krishnas was almost identical to that of the Buddhist traditions: practice detachment, let go of desire, don't get caught up in the drama of life, and the world will reveal itself in a different light. Focus on the Love, and it will set you free.

After chanting and feasting with the rest of the congregation, I realized that the dancing robesman were not brainwashed cultists. In fact, I now understood them to be passionate missionaries, determined to save the planet, and all of its inhabitants, from self-destruction. The same theme found in almost all religions.

As I headed back up the hill to my apartment, it hit me: the realization that wars and conflicts, both large and small, are motivated by guarding one's particular belief – one person's *right,* over another one's wrong. We are, and have been, fighting about differences instead of celebrating similarities. Yes, everyone is different and unique, however, we are more alike than dissimilar.

We all feel pain.

We all need Love.

We all need each other.

CHAPTER 12 PAY NO MIND

"When once you have tasted flight you will always walk the earth with your eyes turned skyward; for there you have been and there you will always be."
-Leonardo da Vinci

On the drive back up the hill I reflected on what I had learned at the center. I was very motivated to get home and meditate. There are thousands of descriptions of meditation. It is like a buffet: there is plenty for everyone, and you can choose what you like. Walking, sitting, eating, chanting, and dancing are only a few ways to meditate. Simply put, meditation is being right here, right now. You could be standing on your head, spinning in circles, and it's a meditation. Anything is a meditation, as long as you are fully present in the moment. Meditation is the art of *becoming one with time and Love.*

Time has only three parts: the past, the present, and the future. Meditation teaches us that the only real place to be is in the present – where love resides. The present may be terrifying, but it is the only thing that really exists. The past is gone, and the future is just a fantasy. Amazingly enough, most humans have honed the art of being everywhere except right here, right now.

Meditation is the key that helps to open up parts of ourselves that have been hidden. We are good at hiding from ourselves and avoiding our shadow. This is dangerous.

When parts of our whole selves are covered up, we ignore emotions such as anger, jealousy, grief, and shame. When ignored these emotions transform and come back into our lives stronger and louder than before. Beware: the next time, they may not be as easily ignored. In the end you have to face yourself.

Taking a deep, long look at yourself won't be easy. It shouldn't be. It takes great courage to see how you have allowed others to influence your life, your actions, and your passions. It takes even greater courage to look at how you have perpetuated this pattern by hurting and trying to influence others. Once we see our whole selves, we can decide what to keep, and what needs tempering.

Meditation gets us to our center, where we need to be. Every problem on our planet is the result of someone not being centered, and as a result, failing to see what is really important: once again, Love. When we lose sight of Love, we lose sight of ourselves. That's when we consider ourselves to be lost.

I began the night's meditation sitting still, taking deep, slow breaths. Deeper. Slower. Each breath took me further into the void. I was breathing through my thoughts, moving past my judgments and opinions – the reputed hallmarks of successful meditation. I let go of control over me, allowing myself to open to and experience the energy in everything.

With each breath I crossed further over the bridge. I did not fear the other side. I feared leaving "me" behind.

Now knee-deep into breathing, I felt the dichotomy of the two me's once again: my *self* and my *soul.* The first lived on this side of the bridge, the second resided somewhere on the far side of the crossing. Tonight the two would be reunited in a new way.

Each time I went into the trance, the traverse across the bridge grew less scary. First I had to let go and forget everything – including trying to recreate the experience I had years ago at the academy. I continued to breathe and apparently was successful in escaping the time-space continuum once again. To this day I don't know how long I was gone, but what happened next shook me for months after.

I died. My body didn't stop working; it was fine when I returned. I mean "died" as in I left this place. Isn't that what death is? Leaving *reality,* whether permanently or temporarily, and experiencing a different *reality?* A shift from one state of consciousness to another? Don't we die each night when we sleep to dream? Are we not reborn the next morning? If death is simply change, then we are dying, *and living,* each second of our existence, forever.

Quickly shaking my head back and forth, I prayed that it would be over and time would start up again. I came out of the meditation rattled, regained my composure, and tried to put words to what I experienced. I was awake for days, spending countless hours writing. Had I truly lost it? No. I had found *it,* and *it* found me. Reunited once again.

Only this time, it was staying.

Days later I would finally find the courage to read the notes from my experience. It was as I suspected. More than just an illusion or a dream, I experienced. The writings before me were the course back to my self – the map back home. The following manuscript pages are the notes from that evening. The *Gamemaster Manual* – the instruction book for being human, and finding Love.

It is my great honor to share this gift with you, and if it has helped, I ask that you share it with others.

May it take you to where you want to be.

Oh...and welcome to *reality!*

REALITY

GAMEMASTER MANUAL

MILLENNIUM EDITION

REALITY
GAMEMASTER MANUAL

Index

A MESSAGE FROM HEADQUARTERS

Created before the dawn of time, It is the first and only game where the player, hero, obstacles, enemy, goal and creator are One. It is changing every second, and has clues everywhere to help you reach the next level (you just have to know how and where to look for them). Filled with terrifying lows and unimaginable highs, It can only be won; there are no ties or losses,

and

It is about to end at any Moment.

Namasté and greetings, Gamemaster. Allow me to be the first to welcome you to your life, or as I call it: *Reality: The Game of Lifetimes.* I see that the instructions have found you. Wonderful! This means only one thing – you are ready to play *reality* as it was meant to be played. Welcome to the *real game!*

This is the official **Millennium Edition** of the *Gamemaster Manual.* There have been many instruction manuals sent to *reality* over the span of time, but many of those have been lost, changed, or destroyed.

You have the manual at a perfect time. In fact, *all time is perfect,* and *so are you.* This version of the game has been going on for a very long time, and will continue to go on forever.

You are experiencing a part of the game. This part, however, is your part. This is your time. You, the player, are one of many in this game, but each and every player is in the game for the same reason: Love. *Reality* is actually the game of Love. You are here to experience *being in Love.*

The *Gamemaster Manual* offers you, the player, the tools necessary to live a life of happiness and joy; this is achieved by noticing the infinite manifestations of Love that are all around you. You are about to master the *reality of Love*. Your reality is about to become ***the reality;*** you are about to be transformed. Your journey toward encompassing Love is about to begin!

You may not remember where you came from or know where you are going, but don't worry, every question will be answered in time. Be patient. Remember, time heals and reveals all things. *It's all just a matter of time.*

You are reading these pages because you are seeking more information about *Reality*. It is necessary to have played *reality* for a few years prior to reading the instructions. You won't understand anything you don't care about. It takes sincere interest to understand *reality*.

If interest is another name for passion, and passion is another name for Love, then to understand Reality, you first have to be willing to *Love reality*. You must Love something completely to completely understand it. With Love, you can understand everything, because Love *is* everything.

Most players search for the meaning of and answers to the game for several years before this book comes into their lives. We treat life – *Reality* – just like any other new toy: only after we've tried playing with it and become frustrated, do we stop to pull out the instructions and read them.

Everyone has experienced the darker sides of *reality*, therefore everyone has the ability to understand it. Love, pain, passion, confusion, grief, sadness, anger, and hate are some of the emotions you must have experienced in order to understand this manual. Without dark, there is no understanding of light, without sour, there is no taste of sweet, and without pain, there is no *appreciation* of Love.

If you have experienced pain, despair, and heartache, you are truly ready to understand the path of the Gamemaster. Had you not gone through your trials blindly bumping into walls and learning the meaning of hardship and challenges, you would not be able to understand the information in this manual. *You must have played the game, to learn the game, to win the game.*

If you spend hours on activities you don't really like, then you are not *Loving time*. You are just watching it as it passes you by. If you are not in Love with the moment, you just pass the time. You let it slip past you. Passing the time is a game where you are giving away everything you have, for nothing. This is one game that a Gamemaster does not play, because a master makes the most of all time.

Time is running out, and so are you. If you are wasting time, you are also wasting Love. You cannot afford to waste either, for each one is a gift. There are many players in *reality* who live life this way: empty, hollow, meaningless. They are not *Loving in time*. They are simply wasting it. For you, that is about to change.

You are about to remember that you are a Gamemaster

What is a Gamemaster? A conscious player who understands the nature and mechanics of *reality,* and uses this understanding to be in, and create, Love. Consciousness is awareness – knowing that you know. It is being able to see past you into the bigger picture.

As a Gamemaster, you are aware that you are here for a limited time and that you must make the most of each second, without sacrificing the next. You are aware of your true nature. You are aware of the game, and the power you have to create or destroy within it.

A Gamemaster embodies the virtues of patience, compassion, and kindness while creating Love. Gamemasters see the world with undaunted eyes, looking past the pain in *reality* to see the Love. We see the beautiful in everything as a child.

This manual will not give you all of the answers you seek. That would be no fun. It will, however, provide you with all the tools you need to find all of the answers. You, the Gamemaster, are responsible for using these tools to find your nature, live in Love, and create happiness.

Best of luck Gamemaster. Remember: be patient, use the force, and look inward for the clues you need to move onto the next level and over the next hurdle. Don't forget that you are actively creating your experience every second. You are here on a mission, and have chosen to be in the game now. Stay alert, relax, breathe, and don't be afraid to ask for help. Everyone needs help: without it, we lose sight of what's truly important. And that, my fellow Gamemasters, is Love.

Now, fasten your seat belt!

-G

THE MISSION

You are alive, and since you are, you are playing *reality*. Living is playing. The game is simple, easy and fun, but can become complicated, difficult, and painful. *Reality, The Game,* or *Life* as some call it, is meant to be experienced as a journey full of challenges and accomplishments, ***not*** a prison sentence or punishment.

The opportunity to feel Love in every moment is inherent in all of us. The reason we are here to play the game of *reality* is to experience Love as often as we can, as intensely as we can, for as long as we can. The combination of *time* and *love!*

We are here to appreciate the intense experience of Love every second. What else is there to live for? If you are not Loving your life, then you are wasting your *time*. Remember, *Love is endless,* however, your time here is limited and is slipping away with each passing moment.

Your first mission in the game: **to be in Love.**

Let's break this down.

To BE: Being is the art of existing in the moment. Staying in the now. For example, if you thought about that idea, then you missed the opportunity to just BE. Thinking is doing, doing is not being. So don't think, just *BE*. To *BE* is to stay clear of all expectations and allow yourself to experience the moment as it is presented to you in *reality*. You experience the moment as it came to you, not as you wish it to be.

In Love: Allowing yourself to feel Love means letting *your true nature* be revealed. You are at one and in Love with yourself, everyone else, and everything around you. Love is the nature of beauty, harmony, balance, and peace. It is the act of surrendering to true intimacy – intimacy within you, and intimacy around you. To BE in Love is to feel Love in all you meet, see, experience, and do. It is letting go of all forms of pain, and allowing yourself to be caressed and kissed by the soul of the one.

Reality is the dance of Love. It is the game where everything is about Love. We look for peace and happiness; that's Love. We try to avoid pain and suffering; they are the absence of Love. Our passions nature of Love. We constantly search for answers and clues about Love. The choice of how to live and play is always up to you, the player. Each moment you can choose to see things as obstacles or opportunities. You have the power to create *reality* as a dream full of Love and hope, or a nightmare filled with chaos and pain. You are making that choice this very second.

You were born with the mystical powers of *creation* and *destruction*. With each decision you make in *reality,* you are either creating Love in your life, or you are destroying it. The decision to create or destroy Love affects everyone around you. Everyone and everything. The things we say, do, and believe all contribute to the active *creation* or *destruction* of Love.

Like in a pool of water, any and every movement and noise you make in *reality* will ripple outward from you in every direction. You affect everything around you. Remember, what comes around goes around, a phenomena often called karma.

As you practice the elements of the Gamemaster, your perception of the game shifts. You become one with the moment, you stand still in the present. You experience life as it is unfolding. It is then that you are truly living. You are at the edge of time as it is being created. In that moment, you are experiencing Love.

A GAMEMASTER IS A BEING IN LOVE

GAME BOARD LAYOUT

The playing board of *reality* is simple. The main goal is to move away from pain and move into Love, or happiness. Any sane person will tell you that they want to live a happy life, with little pain.

A Gamemaster is aware that the direction of the game is always toward Love and away from pain. In everything you think, feel, and do, you create Love. When you experience hardship and pain, do not become angry and destroy more Love. STOP, BREATHE, and search for the clues back to Love. When you see others in pain, remind them of Love. You do this by exuding and creating more Love.

A GAMEMASTER IS THE MESSENGER OF LOVE

PLAYER OPTIONS

1. Play
2. Cheat
3. Pretend
4. Quit

Just like any game on the toy store shelf, *reality* has *only* four playing options: play, cheat, pretend, and quit.

The difference between these options is based solely on your decision to *create* or *destroy* Love at each moment of your *reality*.

1. **Play:** This option is the choice of all Gamemasters, because it is the only option that allows for the *creation* of Love. It is also known as being in Love. With this choice, you yield to the game and play in the moment. Living life on life's terms. You accept events as they unfold and react accordingly. This option is characterized by allowing yourself to be at one with, and aware of, the present moment throughout the experience of *Reality*. Playing the game is also characterized by quickly transforming pain into Love.

There is faith, courage, passion, patience, and Love in the heart of this player.

A note on options 2, 3, & 4:

There are many players who are living in their own worlds, a fantasy or nightmare, aside from *reality*. This phenomenon happens when players experience great pain, and fear future loss of control over the game. Attempting to gain control over the game, and other players in the game, is a reaction to abuse, neglect, and general loss of trust in

Love during their part in the game. *To be in Love* means you are willing to meet the challenges and learn from the lessons that you and *reality* are creating, and the only control you use is keeping your awareness in the present moment. Players who choose the following levels of play refuse to be vulnerable again, and use a great deal of destructive energy to control others in *reality*.

If you have been hurt in *reality*, and you cannot let go of the pain, then you will try to control the game. You will choose options 2, 3, or 4, or any combination of the three because of the need to escape pain in the game. It is ironic that if you resist playing the game *(i.e. options 2,3,4)*, the game becomes more challenging to play. *Reality* will teach you to let go of control at every moment and open your heart to its true nature – Love.

Here are the destructive ways to play the game:

2. **Cheat:** Cheaters are characterized by a lack of patience and tolerance for challenges and pain. Cheaters take power, money, and resources from other players to move their own agenda forward and escape themselves and *reality*. They have given up the belief that *reality* will provide them with what they need *(not want!)*, and tend to feel they deserve more than the gifts they have been presented with, because they do not see the complexity and Love in each present. They feel that they must provide for themselves at the expense of others.

There is no integrity in the heart of this player.

3. **Pretend:** Pretenders are those players who create their own game, or fantasy, within the true game of *reality*. Pretenders are playing two or more games, or agendas, at the same time. Pretenders appear to be actively involved and participating in *reality*. However, behind their complex system of walls and disguises, they are playing according to an entirely different set of rules.

For example, you and some friends are playing a game where the goal is to win all of the money from the other players. You lose a few hands, and believe that there is no way for you to win the game in the end. So, instead of giving up, you create a second game in your mind – in this game you win by *losing* all of your money. Now, in your mind you have won, in *reality*, you have lost. You stopped playing the same game as everyone else. The game you have created is based solely on your rules, game board, and rewards. Keep pretending and playing your personal game and you will become "crazy," meaning you will have lost touch with *reality*.

There is no courage in the heart of this player.

4. **Quit:** This option is exactly what it sounds like: a complete quitting and withdrawal from playing *reality*. Quitters make minimal effort to engage *reality*, if at all. Quitters withdraw from *reality*, become reclusive, and try to remain within the comfort of their surroundings. Simply put, quitters do not care to play anymore. The idea of active participation in the game is replaced with common addictions and other forms of escape. Addictions are nothing more than doing the same thing repeatedly, for long periods of time, thus ignoring the game of *reality* and the players in it. The player who chooses this option is just waiting for *reality* to be over.

There is no passion in the heart of this player.

A GAMEMASTER ALWAYS CHOOSES TO *PLAY* THE GAME

PLAYER MODES

1. Survival Mode
2. Alive Mode
3. Living Mode
4. Gamemaster Mode

In *reality*, there are four main player modes. These modes, again, are based on the ability, or lack thereof, to let go of pain and create Love. Each mode is characterized by the amount of Love and pain a player chooses to create in the game.

I. **Survival Mode:** The player's basic needs are the primary focus in this mode. This level is the most challenging, because the longevity of the player is the main focus. How long the player remains in *reality* depends on how well this level is played. Food, shelter, water, and safety are the main goals of this mode of play, which are necessary to advance to the next level – alive mode. Fun is not a consideration at this level.

Players at this level are mostly in Pain.

II. **Alive Mode:** This mode of play is best characterized by managing all survival mode functions of human existence, plus working and engaging in some social interaction. Players operating in this mode are still playing the game at a minimum, and they use almost no creativity or imagination in finding and making more Love. They are said to feel as if they are barely treading water. The cycle of the alive mode player typically goes: wake up, work, come home, sleep, and start all over again.

Players at this level experience more pain than FUN.

III. **Living Mode:** In this mode of play, the player has mastered all skills of the previous levels and begins to use imagination and creativity to bring happiness and Love into *reality*. Players at this level use tools such as music, art, communication, and other forms of creation to enjoy and create more Love in the game. Emphasis is on *truly living* and *being* in the moment as often as possible. There is still some struggle and lack of complete faith in *reality* at this level.

Players at this level experience more FUN than pain.

IV. **Gamemaster Mode:** At this level, the Gamemaster realizes her or his true nature and uses the tools of *creation* to restore balance, peace, and Love to everyone and everything in the game system. The Gamemaster knows that the first mission of the game is to be in Love, and helps others with this and their own personal missions. The Gamemaster finds Love in everyone and everything. Gamemasters are characterized as having a lack of fear of *reality,* as well as the ability to surpass obstacles with ease and fun. The Gamemaster exudes great confidence in the face of adversity, and fully embodies the virtues of patience, compassion, and kindness throughout their time in *reality*. At this level, pain is realized as a road sign toward Love and is quickly transformed into positive energy.

Players at this level experience only FUN.

A GAMEMASTER IS ALWAYS HAVING FUN

THE LADDER OF LOVE

As we mentioned in Chapter 3, Game Board Layout, our goal as Gamemasters is *to be in Love*. Many players have been burned by Love or just beat down by *reality* in general. When *reality* challenges us, we are actually being called to learn more about ourselves and our true nature. *Reality* also challenges us so we can learn to overcome obstacles for future levels. Both pain and Love are our trainers. Pain, however, trains the player at a *painful speed*. Pain is a road sign in our lives, telling us we have fallen from Love, and instructing us how to return. So, if we are in the pit of despair, in the depths of pain, here is how to return to Love:

You have been transforming pain into Love from the day you were born. In times of complex pain, and fear, it is very easy to lose sight of the way back to Love.

Imagine walking through the woods on a beautiful breezy summer day. You are whistling as you stroll down the woodland path, fully enjoying and being present in the moment. You are in Love.

How do you know? You are content, peaceful, happy, and worry-free. You are not thinking, you are being. That is Love. Suddenly you fall through a covered hole in the ground and crash into the bottom of a pit. What is the best way out? A ladder of course. Shouldn't everyone carry a ladder with them wherever they go? Yes – especially in this game.

To get to the top of any ladder, we must begin with the first step.

Let's see how this works:

Day 1: Imagine that you were just born, and you are now exploring your world. You are curious, so you begin to touch everything. As you go near the stove, your mother yells "DON'T TOUCH THAT!" Do you listen? Probably not. Why? Because we players often like to experience things for ourselves. Our beliefs are formed three ways: from being taught, from observation, or from personal experience. Which of these is the most poignant? If you are one of the curious ones, then personal experience of course. Now, let's say the stove was not on – it wasn't hot when you touched it. What have you learned? Nothing – except the erroneous belief that your mother doesn't know what she is talking about.

Day 2: You have a whole day's worth of experience under your belt, and of course you believe that you know everything there is to know about *reality*. You walk up to the stove and challenge the monster that your mother oh so fears. "I TOLD YOU NOT TO TOUCH THAT!!!" she screams from the wings. Courageously, you throw your cape over your shoulder and engage the steel beast. You touch it, and again it is not on. What have you learned? That your mother is twice as lost as she was yesterday.

Day 3: And you're off. Screaming about the house, touching everything in sight, occasionally putting corner lint and small toy pieces in your mouth. No problem. Until you get to the stove. The drill is the same. You walk up. Mom yells, "DON'T TOUCH THAT!" You touch it, ignoring the panic of your twice-mistaken mentor. Today the stove is on, and it's HOT. You get burned. Burn = PAIN. Now you realize that you have made a big MISTAKE. MISTAKES are what we call the complete experience of PAIN. The lesson is not over, you have only traveled up the first two parts of the ladder: PAIN ➤MISTAKE.

Day 4: Today is different. In fact, *very different.* A great lesson is about to unfold. As you come near the stove you take a quick turn toward the toy chest and avoid the stove altogether. Does your mom need to say anything? Not at all. The Ladder of Love has done its job. As you walked near the stove you remembered the EXPERIENCE from yesterday, and it made you WISE to the dangers of the stove. Today you experience HAPPINESS, a degree of LOVE, because you did not get burned. HOORAY!!

You have successfully learned to climb up the ladder. You are HAPPY because you had the WISDOM to avoid getting burned again by the stove. That WISDOM was based on your EXPERIENCE with the stove, but not just any experience: it was the MISTAKE you made with the stove the day before which taught you the most. You called it a MISTAKE, because you were burned. That burn caused you PAIN. Thank you PAIN for teaching me not to go near the stove. But remember, you will see that stove many times again in your life, only next time it may look different.

Isn't it amazing how the ladder works? Even more amazing is that you have been using this ladder all of your life. Sometimes you climb it quickly, sometimes slowly. Either way, you have always been climbing it.

Could you have avoided the whole thing? Yes, by using the other two learning styles – teaching and observation. Your mother *taught* you not to touch the stove. You just didn't listen. Had you stood near the stove long enough you might have *observed* someone else getting burned. But no, you had to *experience* it for yourself. Good for you!

Now if anyone asks about the stove, you know what you are talking about. Besides, we are here to experience *reality,* not just hear about it, or watch it pass by. Now you know what to do when you get burned and next time you see the stove – learn from it.

So what do you do with the PAIN, now that you have moved up the ladder to LOVE?

LET IT GO.

This is a crucial move in the game. Let PAIN go. If you are holding onto PAIN, you are living in the past. The game is played in the present, remember. Living in the past causes more PAIN. After you let the MISTAKE and the PAIN go, you add the EXPERIENCE to your memory banks of life's WISDOM. If later in life you are faced with a similar challenge, you have tools to meet that challenge successfully and advance to the next rung of the ladder – LOVE.

The main reason players do not let go of PAIN is because PAIN sometimes leaves behind *shame, guilt,* and *fear.* These emotions are really PAIN in disguise. If you hold on to them, you are really holding onto PAIN.

PAIN is the only thing that prevents a player from moving up the ladder.

A GAMEMASTER KNOWS HOW TO RETURN TO LOVE

SKYDIVING THE TIME-SPACE CONTINUUM

Reality is brought to you in part by the time-space continuum. Time is a measurement and constantly moving. As time unfolds, so does space. Time and space change everything. The game is always changing. *reality* is in a constant state of change within the theater of time and space. Nothing stands still. Nothing. Everything is always moving, growing, and transforming.

Without getting into the physics and science of time and space, there are only a few things you *need* to know. Time exists in three places: past, present, and future. We know this because that is how our consciousness swings through time – from the past, to the present, to the future, to the present, past, and over again. Back and forth, all day long.

Time is like a pendulum, constantly swinging. Notice that if you let it swing, it will spend more time in the past and future, than in the present.

Only the present moment is *reality.*

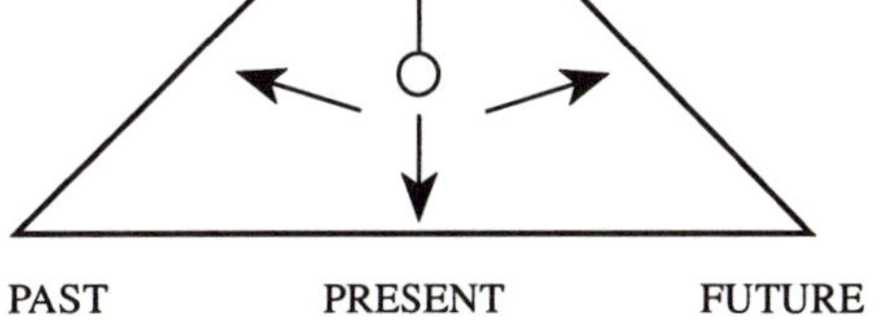

The most important time in *reality* is now. Poof! You just missed it. Thinking about it means you tried to grab it. When we try to hold on to time, or things in time, we are missing now. The challenge of the game is to stay present. Holding on is doing, and doing is not being. The only way to prepare for the future is to be in the now – the closest place to the future you can get. If we worry about the future, we are missing where we are really at. As many in *reality* have already said, "The moment right now is a gift from the universe, and that's why they call it the present."

This very moment is the one place in the game that the player has any control – control of their actions in and awareness of, the ever present moment.

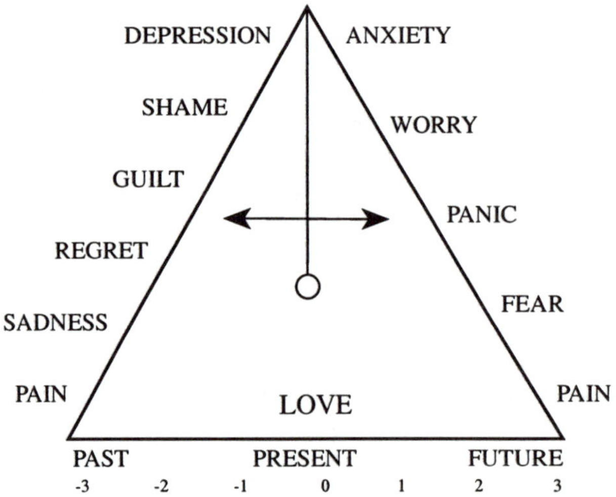

Emotions tell us where we are, and where we want to be. Time is the keeper of emotions. Emotions are based in time. If you spend too much time in the past, sadness, grief, shame, regret, and guilt will become your *reality*. All of these emotions *slow down* time. The events that caused these emotions have passed. They are in the past. You cannot do anything more with them except let them go, heal, and move on.

If you spend too much time in the future, fear, worry, panic, and anxiety become your *reality*. All of these emotions *speed up* time. The imagined events that cause these emotions have not yet happened and may never happen. Although you created the imagined fears in the future, you cannot do anything more with them now than to stay present, and let them go.

To avoid these negative emotions, or at least to keep them to a minimum, try to keep the pendulum at zero – NOW – in the present.

The only place that *reality* is happening. The true home of Love.

Remember that *emotions* are the *compass of the soul.*

How do we continue to stay in Love with the present? How do we avoid missing it by not thinking about it? Some great ways to help this process are meditation, breathing, tai chi, yoga, sports, dance, music, and so on. There are many ways to practice mindfulness; find one that fills your soul and ignites your *passion*. Don't look outside yourself for passion, because it is already in you. It has been. The goal is to still the mind, through passion of the moment, and quiet the noise inside so that you can hear the symphony of *reality*.

A GAMEMASTER IS PASSIONATE ABOUT THIS VERY MOMENT

DETACHMENT

The opposite of attachment is detachment. Detachment means to let go. Detachment is a key component in the path of the Gamemaster. Its most important contribution is as a tool that allows us to let go and BE in the ever-present moment.

Oftentimes players miss the opportunity to move on to the next challenge, a higher state of fulfillment, because they are holding onto something, missing the moment, thus skipping over important information or clues. In other words, *not paying attention to reality* – the *only* fee required for playing *The Game*. Players who cannot or will not detach are too preoccupied with, and chained to, the past or the future. When we let go of yesterday and tomorrow, the last hour and the next second, we allow ourselves to move on through time and be now in the game.

The only way to become comfortable with letting go or detaching from wants, desires, pain, and relationships with other players is to practice it. One way to practice detachment is through creation. Spend a few hours engaging in one of your many *passions*. If you don't know what they are, find them. Cook, paint, do a puzzle. When you have completed your passion, and the work is done, take it back apart, throw it away, or give it as a gift.

Spread the Love.

Pour the puzzle back into the box. Give the dinner to a homeless person. Use the painting for gift wrap. Let it go and be happy that you were there and alive to create it. After you bid your creation well, and send it on its way, let it go. Return to the moment. Don't think about the time it took you to complete your creation, or the effort you expended. Those are the *illusions of the past.* Stay in the now. Remember, we are always in a permanent state of temporary change. Holding on wastes time, and *it's all just a matter of time.*

A GAMEMASTER KNOWS WHEN TO LET GO

THE EMOTIONAL RELEASE

Heavy or negative emotions, which are every one except Love, create tears. Tears are the sweat glands of the heart – the breath of our soul. When you allow yourself to cry, you release a weight which slows you down and keeps you from living in the present. Like sandbags anchoring a hot air balloon to the Earth, trapped tears anchor you to the nightmare, preventing you from rising out of the ashes into the beauty of peace, balance, and true Love.

Understand, process, and let go. That is the way we release ourselves from the chains of pain, and move up The Ladder of Love. So many of us keep our pains trapped in our hearts, essentially suffocating our souls. We may do this because we feel shameful, guilty, scared, or wrong. When pain enters the heart, at some point it *must be released.*

Players do not move on in life and may become depressed, anxious, and desperate because they do not cry. The heart and soul react to every event of loss and trauma. *Reality* has its good parts and challenging, or what some call "bad," parts. We easily tell people about the good parts, and find that the good stuff is pretty easy to deal with. It's the challenging parts, the loss and trauma of life's events, that we sometimes don't know what to do with. What should you do? Cry.

When we experience pain, our mind and emotions process it

and try to release the rest. Pain goes into our minds, then to our hearts, and up to our tear ducts. We have three choices at this point:

1. Cry: This is when the player allows the soul and heart to breathe. Pain gets processed into tears, and crying is the physical release of the excess pain. We all have the need to cry, just as we need to sweat and breathe. No one is excluded from this rule. NO ONE! This action is necessary to successfully play Reality. A player who can cry feels:

At peace, balanced, and lighter

If we decide we don't want to let the pain go, and try to *control* the natural process of releasing tears, we find that two more difficult situations arise: we either *explode* or *shut down.*

Remember that as a Gamemaster, you try to control *nothing* except awareness and reactions in the present moment. When we try to control *reality,* and our tears in *reality,* we create resistance to the natural law of things, and induce more pain.

2. Explode: If you hold in your tears long enough, you may find that at one point you can't control yourself any longer. KABOOM! You explode. When you encounter a moment of minor emotional release, the floodgates you built for so long collapse. You lose it. Whether through the energy of anger or severe depression, you explode and have even less control over the acting out of the pain.

Imagine that you have kept in a pain for a very long time. Each day you felt the pressure build, and you worked hard to keep back the tears, by adding more bricks to your wall of pain. Now, millions of gallons of pain have been blocked by your dam. The wall is growing weak.

One day your friend walks up to you and tells you your shoe is untied. KAPOW! You lose it. That easy. You fall down crying – or worse. You have now *exploded.* You have lost complete control of your behaviors at this point. A player that has allowed themselves to *explode* feels:

Embarrassed and humiliated

If we repress our natural process of release and letting go, and can resist the *explode* stage, we may find ourselves at shut down.

3. Shut Down: If a player holds in tears for too long, the tears, as well

as the player, get backed up. The tears grow stale and bitter within the tear ducts. The player at shut down has held in the tears for so long that now they won't come out. This player is beyond *explode* and at system shut down – clogged pipes. This is not good: the system has backed up so much that it is now stuck. The heart attempts to break down the excess of tears through other, usually self-destructive, ways. The body can die when it goes into shut down. The heart can as well: when we feel our hearts die, we call it depression. If you are at shut down, then you have also opted to quit. There is no motivation to live. You are ready to give up. A player at shut down feels:

Hopeless, powerless, empty, and dead inside

The key to moving up The Ladder of Love is healing the pain. This applies to all of life. When we hold on to pain, we fear. When we fear, we run. When we run, we are not playing the game.

You are here to play reality, not run from it.

A GAMEMASTER IS NOT AFRAID TO CRY

AWARENESS

Awareness is living without the blinders – the blinders we have created and the ones that have been created for us. Awareness is being mindful of all that is in you and around you. Being aware is playing *reality* and observing you playing *reality* at the same time. You are you and not you at once. You see what was, is, and will be. Because your eyes are wide open, you are ready for anything life throws at you.

Cultivating awareness is easy. Sit in a room quietly for a bit. Notice the silence, the stillness. Now, ring a bell once, and follow its sound with your ears. Notice how the sound doesn't suddenly stop: it rings and rings itself into silence. It is a gradual and smooth transition into nothing. This is how we should listen to life – carefully, quietly, and thoroughly, until it is finished teaching us what it has to teach us.

Often, we easily get bored and agitated, and stop the ringing ourselves, or just walk away. We put the bell down, and pick up something else that makes noise. As a Gamemaster, you listen patiently, with awareness of every vibration, until it's finished with you.

There are always opportunities to practice awareness and mindfulness. As you eat, chew until you cannot taste the flavor. As you breathe, notice every ounce of air as your lungs wax and wane. As you live, notice the beauty that is dancing around you.

Through awareness, we discover the incredible and amazing orchestra of the cosmos.

A GAMEMASTER IS AWARE

THE LIVING GAMEMASTER

Is a Gamemaster someone who has no pain in her or his life? Someone who dances on clouds and walks on water? Of course not! It's you! Someone who knows how *The Game* is played, and who is aware of how to transform pain into potential. A player who knows how, and where, to find Love.

A Gamemaster is always aware that the goal is to *be in Love*. Do they make mistakes? Absolutely. Remember, without pain and mistakes, you cannot climb up The Ladder of Love.

You have now learned the basic tools needed to find all of the answers to win *The Game*. There is a new light on your day and the way you live it. There will be times when you forget, and feel that you are lost. Great! There is a lesson there, too. Don't run from it, just be, and stay open to learning what *your soul **and** reality* are trying to teach you.

Reality is always sending you lessons about Love. Always.

Reality is cyclical. We move from easy periods, to challenging ones, back to easy ones. The trick is to enjoy the easy and stay on top of the challenging ones.

As you continue to play *reality,* you choose the degree to which you feel and experience *The Game*. It has, is, and will always be recommended that you make the most of the experience, and feel *reality* to the fullest. If you're happy, feel the happiness to its fullest. If you are tired, be tired; surrender to that feeling. If you are sad, be sad. Allow yourself to be. In time all things will pass.

Resistance of experiencing this very moment to the
fullest extent only delays the inevitable –
your growth.

Love brought you into this world. Love will escort you out. When you die, you return to Love. Love drives you. Love confuses you. It is Love you hunger for. As a Gamemaster, your job is to enjoy *reality* and the dance of Love, while contributing to Love's creation. You don't want to mess the place up without helping to clean it up, now do you? *What if you have to return at some point?*

Winning the game is simple. The measurement of a winner is not how much you have Loved over the course of your life, but how passionately you are Loving – everything – this very second.

As you master the tools of the manual, magic and purpose will become a common part of your everyday experience. Get ready! They are signs that you are on the path. The greatest sign may be a feeling that your nightmare is being transformed into a beautiful story as you originally dreamt it. Creation and transformation are hallmarks of the Gamemaster. You are capable *and responsible* for both.

The rules are easy to follow, and the codes to win are simple. It is the practice that takes some work. How challenging your experience of *The Game* will be depends on how much resistance you create against the moment.

Each moment is only that – a moment.
Live it.
Be it.
Love it.

If you really want to be happy, following the rules and practicing will be easy. If you are not sure you are ready to be happy, then place this manual back on your shelf or give it away. But don't worry, it will be back.

You will always reach your dreams and goals. It's inevitable. This is because it serves not just you, but all of *reality*. You are part of *the game*, and it is a part of you.

When you are happy, so is *reality*. You only have a slight idea of the best way to get to the next chapter of your journey and reach greater states of happiness and harmony. The universe *knows* the best way! Remember, the way you get to your next goal will *never* be the way you want it to be. And also don't forget, the Goddess does in fact have a very big sense of humor.

Enjoy each day. As you cultivate and create Love in the hearts of others, your own Love and life will flourish from dormant seeds into a field of heavenly flowers. You are about to be in constant bloom.

Welcome to *Reality...*
For tomorrow you begin the day as

A
Gamemaster

A GAMEMASTER knows there will always be something
new to master...
F o r e v e r

The Theory

Everyone alive owns a theory to life,
which tells us how to live, who to love, what to like;
It tells us when to laugh and when we should cry,
how things were born, and why they must die.

This theory is our own grand vision of life,
its values help distinguish between day and night.
We are passengers on the coaster of nature's flight,
we use our clear conscience, and try with all might.

Our travels may appear to confine us to ground,
regardless, our search for life's crown will be found;
as we pray to become our hopes and our dreams,
the purpose of life is to be happy it seems.

Vocatus adque non vocatus, Deus aderit

(Called or not called, God is present.)
- *C.G. Jung*

God is a DJ

-Faithless

GAMEMASTER REVIEWS

"A true work of destiny. There is no doubt in my mind that Rob Jacoby was destined to write this book, giving us all a glimpse into our own personal futures. I found the book impossible to put down because it somehow felt like I was being given the keys to my own destiny. It will be recommended reading to all my students because of its passion and possibility."

KC Miller – Founder, Instructor
Southwest Institute of Healing Arts
Scottsdale, Arizona

"**GAMEMASTER** is an intriguing and compelling discussion of some remarkably simple yet profound ideas. Though the metaphor of a game is used throughout the **GAMEMASTER**, Rob Jacoby constantly points beyond games to the central concept: it's all about Love. I heartily recommend it."

Rick Doblin, Ph.D. – Author, Lecturer

"In a search for truth, you could read volumes of spiritual texts or you can pick up this amazing man's story of his own mystical revelation and the accompanying **GAMEMASTER MANUAL.** You will learn how to play the game of life and win, how to create freedom from pain, turn mistakes into wisdom, and reconnect with the passion that comes from living life in the present. Never have I seen mystical wisdom so simply and eloquently shared."

Ann Albers – Author, Spiritual Instructor

"The **GAMEMASTER** is a moving life story filled with the usual and something very extra. This extra was the innovation for the **GAMEMASTER MANUAL** which helps you create your very next life experience except you do it consciously, intertwining reality with love."

Susan B. Ward M.D., President – The Consciousness Institute
Exton, Pennsylvania

"...very well written and readable...takes the best of spiritual philosophies and transforms them into a twenty-first century set of rules that everyone is familiar with in their daily lives..."

Richard Forno – Author, Lecturer
Coauthor: "The Art of Information Warfare"

"**GAMEMASTER** provides a fascinating reading experience. Many of the principles outlined in this book can be applied to psychotherapy. All of the principles can be applied to life."

Kathy A. Caruso, Psy.D. – Psychotherapist

"Rob Jacoby has done an interesting thing: he has created a book that is both easy to read and thought-provoking. His life and job give you a great set-up, and his **GAMEMASTER MANUAL** allows you to conceptualize a manner of living life more fully. His book clarifies the game of life and provides many useful suggestions to reach Love and avoid some all too common pitfalls. I think mental health workers would greatly appreciate Jacoby's insights and perspectives."

Scott Wells Browning, Ph.D. – Associate Professor of Psychology
Chestnut Hill College

"In **GAMEMASTER,** Robert Jacoby, in his effervescent, humorous, uplifting style, has given us a sure-fire process of living life to the fullest by overcoming obstacles, shaking off those 'demons' that possess our inner selves, putting us on the path to happiness. He gives us the key to unlock the true reality within each of us. He skillfully explores the meaning of love, 'the universal constant,' and delves into the similar spiritual qualities of the world's religions and, in an introspective analysis, shows us the way through love to achieving inner peace and contentment with ourselves and each other."

Alfred Sanelli – Brigadier General, PAARNG (Ret)
Chaplain, Valley Forge Military Academy & College

"**GAMEMASTER** is health food for the soul. It is a way to nurture, develop and maintain your emotional well being and sense f self. Definitely a must-read if you want to live a life filled with peace, love and happiness."

Nelson Bosque, MBA – Senior Account Executive
Loomis Fargo & Co.

"Though **GAMEMASTER** is a book written by a talented and loving writer, it is actually a message that the Universe has been trying to send us since the beginning of time. I am glad that we all have the pleasure of reading it in this form."

Brandon Woll – 1 LT, U.S. Army
Military Intelligence

"Wonderful...simple yet profound. A MUST read for anyone on a spiritual journey. The message will stay with you long after you have finished the last page. We are so fortunate to have access to such an exciting talent as Rob Jacoby."

Phyllis C. Osisek, M.A. – Director of Counseling Services
Ursinus College, Collegeville, PA

"Rob Jacoby's paradigm of how to play the game of life is tremendously appealing to those of us who want to be happy and like to 'keep it simple, stupid.' His emphasis on being responsible for your individual choices evaporates the blame we tend to give others for our particular misery. He encourages the reader to be a 'player' in reality and teaches him the steps to become a Gamemaster – someone who 'exudes great confidence in the face of adversity, and fully embodies the virtues of patience, compassion, and kindness.' **GAMEMASTER** is a quick, easy read that intrigues, fascinates, instructs, and, finally, has the reader slapping his forehead and saying, "Why didn't I think of life this way?" This book will help many people overcome obstacles on their way to being happy, positive people."

Samuel H. Wrightson, Jr. Ed.D. – LTC, USA (Ret)
Assistant Dean, VFMC

"**GAMEMASTER** is not just a book but a philosophy of how to live life. It puts into perspective what is important and describes a vast array of emotions that we all experience yet cannot begin to describe. Rob Jacoby is able to identify and draw such a clear and beautiful picture of the very thoughts and feelings we all have yet can't articulate. Rob is a rare and genuine soul that I have the pleasure of knowing and respecting both personally and professionally."

Pattie O'Connor, M.A., CISW
Clinical Manager